I0614972

Charles J. Pickering

The last David

And other Poems

Charles J. Pickering

The last David
And other Poems

ISBN/EAN: 9783337111137

Printed in Europe, USA, Canada, Australia, Japan

Cover: Foto ©Andreas Hilbeck / pixelio.de

More available books at **www.hansebooks.com**

AND OTHER POEMS.

' Wel I wot, that ye han herbiforne
Of makynge ropen, and lad awey the corne ;
And I come after, glenying here and there,
And am ful glad yf I may fynde an ere
Of any goodly worde that ye han left.'

CHAUCER.

LONDON :

ELLIOT STOCK, 62, PATERNOSTER ROW, E.C.

1883.

CONTENTS.

THE LAST DAVID.

PERSONS.

ZEDEKIAH, *King of Judah.*

ELISHAMA, *an old Counsellor.*

GEDALIAH, *a young Noble.*

NERGAL SHAREZER, *Babylonish General.*

Warder, old Servant of the Kings.

Eunuch of King Zedekiah.

NAOMI, *a Prophetess.*

Messengers, Soldiers.

Scene : East Wall of Jerusalem, adjoining the Temple. *Time :* Night (of the last day of the eighteen months' siege in the last year of the last King of Southern Palestine).

' What if even the rod which despiseth shall be no more ?'

WARDER (*alone*).

WEARY am I, and heartsick. Night and day
Rolls on the din of battle, and the air
Is thick with cries of slaughter at the walls,
And death-groans in the streets, where the blue
  famine
Strikes down our people hourly, and plague runs
Through thin ranks of defenders, as a flash
Of lightning rending loftiest cedars down.
And worse than all, that bane of all our hope,
Unceasing faction surging to and fro,
Whereon our ship of state is shattered, till
Her rent sides gape on ruin. If but he
That guides her now, were hearted like his sire,
Not tossed in tempest, but on calmer waters
And in a harbouring quiet, would we ride,
Fenced from disaster by the shadowing wing
Of the great eastern eagle. Never yet
Have we seen peaceful seasons, prosperous days :

Rich cornfields blooming golden, olive-groves
Heavy with fruit, and teeming palm and vine,
And multitudinous congregations streaming
Through our fair streets, all tending Templeward—
Not one without his offering, firstling fat
And spotless, meet for holy festival—
Since Lord Josiah perished in his prime.
Ah! then was mourning, when the messenger
Came panting from the far-off field, and shouted,
Not loudly, but with choking voice, as he
Neared the high gate, that opened as he came,
' The King is fallen !'   And the cry, caught up
By them within, flew like the wildfire, on
Through the broad city to the Temple walls,
And hung on Hinnom valley like a cloud.
Then from each house the shriek of women rose
And children, wailing for the fallen ; for he
Was dear to us, and precious ; and Jehovah
Had dowered him with a gladness and a strength
Far past his fathers.   Happy was the land
Beneath him, when he ruled it in his prime,
Sweeping out old corruption that had eaten
Into the people like disease, adorning
Anew the holy places, that for years
Had lain neglected and untrod.   Even now
Through this mirk night-gloom I can see the shapes
Of heathen altars whereon one time rose

The stream of sacrifice to Chemosh, Milcom,
Ashtaroth, and their crew, when worshippers
Thronged to them, aye, and from our sacred city,
Now rubbish heaps of ruin whereupon
Foul worms crawl, and the night-bird winds her horn
At midnight. All this did that King of ours
Whom would that high Jehovah had preserved
To be our guardian still! But woe is me!
What boots it to be dreaming, ever dreaming
Of the past days, days that were once so sweet,
When all the bitter hail of strong destruction
Is raining on our heads?

      I hear a hum
Of voices as in supplication, rise
From out the Temple depths, and there streams off
A cloud of incense, scenting all the air,
Wafted by sea winds eastward over me ;
And footsteps as of some one springing softly
Up the high steps, come nearer.—Who art thou?

EUNUCH.

No fierce Chaldee, but only the King's eunuch !—
Yet stay, old man, and hear me. Our sad lord,
Broken in spirit and well-nigh despairing,
Has gone once more to sacrifice and pray
I' th 'Temple yonder, hoping still 'gainst hope
To win some cheering token. Even now

I see him coming hither, and with him
A lordling whom methinks thou knowest well.

(They pass aside; enter KING *and* GEDALIAH
speaking.)

GEDALIAH.

Think on thy people ; they are dying off
By scores, with, war and want, and pestilence :
With war, that only lasts while Zedekiah
Fears to send out a messenger of peace ;
With want, that would pass over like a cloud
In summer, were his spirit good to yield
Our pledged allegiance once again, and see
Corn pouring in our portals for the people ;
With pestilence, that walks abroad unchecked
While famine-stricken corpses strew our streets,
And there are none to bury them.—Oh, thou
Who art this people's shepherd and their King,
Have pity on them, and tear off that veil
Of clinging death that binds them, so their eyes
May look upon the light of life again :
So will they bless thy name, and children's children
Remember thee with love, as him who erred,
But yet unwittingly, and turned once more,
To the right path, long years before he died,
And prospered after, all his days.

KING.

My soul
Is weary, and I fain would sleep.   Thy words
I hear not, but mine eyes can see thee pleading,
And doubt not but it is the same old cry
For weak submission to a wearied foe.
What wouldst thou have me do?   Surrender me,
My wives, my mother, children, household, all
To ravishers, who will laugh me to scorn—
Egged on by them that traitorously forsook me—
And make me a mere by-word to my neighbours
Of Ammon, Moab, Edom ; and proud Tyre
Will dance upon her ocean rock, exulting
That the third branch of him who brought to shame
Her cherished idols, and whose influence spread
Like a broad cedar over all the land,
Is fallen.   Never will I yield to this.

GEDALIAH.

Dead mayst thou be to pity, but to shame
No son of David's line was dead before.

KING.

What shame?   What greater shame could be, than that
     that
A king of Judah, after wearying
His enemy long time with fruitless siege,
Should tamely yield him at the eleventh hour?

GEDALIAH.

A shame, a greater shame by thousand-fold,
Clings to thee now : thou swarest by Jehovah
To peace and. fealty, when the Lord of Babel
Steadied thy throne for thee, what time the boy
Jehoiachin—a young and tender boy,
Warm from his mother's breast, compelled to rule—
Went weeping with the men of Babel home ;
A solemn covenant thou tookst, to be
The friend of Babel alway, and the foe
Of Egypt—but thy pride deluded thee
Like thy false brother, and the rotten reed
Was clung to, snapping short, as it did ever ;
And oaths and promises were flung to the wind.
But though he is wronged deeply, the great King
Is no hard dealer, and will spare thy land
And this fair city and thyself, if only
Thou bend down thy proud soul, and send him
    peace.

KING.

I hear thee, son of Shaphan, and I heed thee.
Leave me awhile, so I may ponder over
The words thou hast spoken—bitter words, but
    true.   (*Partly aside.*)

GEDALIAH.

May He that sits in heaven above breathe in thee
A spirit of peace and fair humility !   [*Exit·*

KING.

True are his words : I felt them cleave my soul
Like keenest arrows—so they rankle now.
Ay, oaths are not forgotten, when vain men
Have trod them underfoot, by Him whose name
They took, and hallowed were withal. Oh, often
Has my heart smitten me for that perjury !
But maybe 'tis too late now for repentance,
And hope is past, is gone ? And I must go
Down to the grave unhonoured, and unwept ;
Sped by my people's curses to the home
Of shadows, mighty once, 'mong whom the worm
Crawls, and the spectral owl shrills evermore !
No, no, it cannot be ! It shall not be !
The heart in me is changed. Death to old pride,
And life for Zedekiah and his people !—
A messenger !—Ho, warder, run and tell
                    (*Warder comes forward.*)
Lord Gedaliah that the King would see him ;
Thou'lt find him in the Temple-court. Haste, haste !
                    [*Exit Warder.*
—Yet, yield myself into the hand of him
Who has but cause enough to hate me, put
Me to foul shame, and call mine enemies round,
That they may see the friendless King of Judah
Made sport for them to bark about, like dogs
About a wounded lion ?—Oh, the gall

Of servitude—it presses me !   And yet
'Tis not too late, even now, to change my will,
Fling craven cringing to those dogs that love it,
And put my honour on, robe-like, again !
But if he take the city ?   If he starve
The warriors to submission, would not he,
The proud, stone-hearted captain, stung to rage
By his long baffling, cast Jerusalem
Into the gulf of ruin, and my house
Raze out of life, as if they ne'er had been ?
I know not !—maybe fearful 'twere to know.
A thousand times would I that I had never
Been born, to hurl an innocent boy to ruin,
And on the shattered remnant of his throne
Sit like a carrion bird, exulting.   There
I fell ; contented, no, not with the lot
Of highest in all Judah, save the King,
And trusted by him with his inmost counsels—
For he, poor boy ! would often come to me,
Beseeching that his uncle dear would guide him
In this new project of a stripling's brain—
Moreover, till his fall, the people loved me,
And never, as I galloped through the streets
At morning, with my chosen company,
Did I see any face that scowled at mine
As men scowl now ; but every son of Adam
I passed and greeted, greeted me with smiles,

And called Jehovah's blessing on my head.
They called me fair—I was not furrowed then
And grey—and fairest maidens cast on me
Their looks of love, and murmured sweetest ' Hail !'
Flinging their lily-garlands, dewy-fresh,
About my horses' necks ; and some rare bloom
They would go out at dawn to search for, toss
Into my car, with all their tender might,
And weave them simple songs, wherein my name
Rang often, in low tones that filled the heart
That heard them with deep joy.   Fool that I was,
To leave all this for factious, traitorous plotting,
'Gainst him who only joyed to see my joy !
Fool ?   Worse than fool !—for if this day he is not,
Upon my head will rest that guiltless blood
No sacrifice can purge me of.   Had I
Been born a lowly man, and gained scant fare
By keeping others' sheep, and lain the nights
On the cold grass, beneath the dew of heaven,
Methinks this crushing care had never come
To stifle me, and peaceful days were mine,
Heart free from sin-stain, life from shame ; but now
The heavy morrow like a storm-dark sea
Surges before me, and casts bitter foam
That tastes like tears, into my eyes, the foretaste
Of sharper ills to come.   When the young lord
I tarry for comes at my bidding, sure

That I have called him but to take to the walls
Our meek submission, shall I say him nay?
The oracles are mute—but yet no sign
Of evil did they give—maybe no answer
Meant good in store, but hidden from all eyes!
Yet, should the people rise up in rebellion
And cast me out—they love me, no, not one—
Perchance exalting this same Gedaliah
To be their head, and treat for them with Babel,
'Twere not so well!   To yield were better far—
If yield in time—and time is speeding swift——

(*Enter* ELISHAMA.)

ELISHAMA.

My lord the King alone here, on the walls?—
I have been searching for thee long, but dark
The night is, and I met no one had seen thee.
Bear'st thou a braver heart than yesterday?

KING.

Why question me?   There is no cause for change?
The heavens are black above us, and our fate
So lowers before us, dark and answerless.

ELISHAMA.

Better than divination is good cheer;
Better than signs and tokens is the hope
That wavers not with waiting, never sinks
Crossing the bitter waters of ill-hap.

Keep up thy heart, oh King! Though now all
    heaven
Be black, the morning will come presently ;
This midnight of our fortunes cannot bide
For ever, and the sun-blaze and blue day
Will rise upon us surely, if we wait.

KING.

Waited full long have we, and yet the foe
That presses us seems fresh and fair as when
He first threw up his over-peering bastions
Against our walls, and trained his engines on,
And ranged his trampling thousands in the plain
Before our gate ; and when we looked on and saw
The gleaming whites of thrice ten thousand eyes
Dart hate at us, and slaughter.—Well know I
That tireless foe will yet outwait us all.

ELISHAMA.

This craven heart of thine will be the ruin
Of fair Jerusalem yet, if all my words
But set the text for bodings of despair.
Think'st that thy fathers never felt the weight
Of weary waiting for a help that came not,
And afterward laughed at their coward fears ?—
When young Jehoram, of the house of Omri,
Whose Tyrian mother's blood runs in thy veins,
Swayed in Samaria, Syrian Ben-Hadad—
Old was he then, the wine-bibber Ben-Hadad—

Thought to beleaguer him, as years before
He did his father Ahab ; and marched out
From green Damascus, his rich paradise,
With thousands, many thousands, men of war
And chariot warriors, and laid closest siege
To lone Samaria in the hills.   Days passed,
And weeks, and months, and nigh a score of months;
And darkened in Samaria every eye.
Then strong men sank with famine, and a moan
Of dumb despair went up to heaven, when corn
Was wholly spent, and through the streets at noon
Went wild-eyed women, fresh from their dark feast,
And wailing for the babes that were not.   Men
Looked up to the blue heaven then, and doubted
Whether Jehovah kinged it there or no.
It fell one evening, as the twilight grew
Deeper and deeper, and the stars were born,
Four lepers sat within the southern gate.
Worn down with hunger and their foul disease
They only waited death ; when suddenly
One, starting up, with frenzy in his look,
Shrieked out : ' Why sit we here until we die ?
Let us go seek the Syrians : they have food ;
If they should spare us, then we live indeed ;
If they should slay us, then we can but die.'
And through the fallen night they took their way
Down the long hill and over miles of valley

And reached the Syrian outposts, where they
    thought
To be seized on, and brought before the King
For life or death—but all was wondrous still :
' The watchmen slumber,' thought they; ' it is well.'
And they pressed on still farther, through that camp
Of numberless pavilions, breathing odour
From scented silken curtains, but so still
And death-like, that their wonder numbed their
    pain ;
Still they went on, till at the uttermost verge
Of the great camp they turned, and saw that none
Was in its bounds, of man.   Then hunger came
And drove them raging to the hoarded food
In those rich tents, whose ivory tables bore
The priceless weight of jewelled goblets, full
For feasting, of the odorous wine of Lebanon,
Whereon they fed ; and with returning life
Came greed, and tempted them with the fine gold
And gem-inwoven draperies, and rich arms
Strewn on the earth about them ; so they took
Each what he counted costliest, and hid
In the rock-clefts.   Then hurried they again
To high Samaria, and the gate-ward told
How that the Syrian camp was empty, still,
With horses tied, and asses, but no one
Of all their foes.   The gate-ward told the King

Who, roused at midnight, held it but a snare
Set by the Syrians to entrap the city,
Yet sent his messengers to see. They came
And saw, and witnessed to their lord again
That all was true. Then rose the famished people
With one strong shout of gladness, and ran out
To the camp to plunder wheat and barley, till
The city flowed with plenty.

KING.

Is it told

Why in such haste the Syrians left their store ?

ELISHAMA.

'Tis even so. The King of Judah came
By cover of darkness, with his men of war,
And fell on them, unready as they were,
And chased them through the many-folded hills
To the bank of Jordan by Beth-barah's ford ;—
And it is said moreover in the record,
That Lord Jehovah made the welkin ring
With din of chariots, and with tramp of horses,
As of a mighty host ; and panic seized
The men of Hamath, ere Jehosaphat
Fell with his chosen champions on their midst.
So waited King Jehoram, and so found
The fruit of patient waiting. So do thou.

KING.

Old man, thy tale is fair ; but what one King

The Last David.

Is there, who would fall, full of victory
Bought for him by triumphant angel armies,
On this Sharezer, captain of all hosts
Which the great King has warring in the west,
Master of all the delegated power
Of him who sways our fortunes, as a god
His wand ?   Where is the King of Judah now ?
Samaria, and all Israel, desolate
These hundred years and more—and Salem,
Our father David's city, which he won
From strong Araunah and his people, all
Men of war-sinew, laughing in their strength,
But yet from even them he reft it, made
His high home here, and hallowed to Jehovah
The city for an endless heritage—
This glory-haunted stronghold of our fathers
Lies at a stranger's mercy, and her King,
Like a caged lion, pent in narrow bounds,
Frets ever at the death before his eyes.
I will hear hope no more.

ELISHAMA.

                 Lo, I am old ;
Full eighty years have I kept passover,
And longer much I do not think to live ;
But, by mine age, and by my hoary hairs,
And by this white beard, that has never known
The touch of shameful fingers, and these eyes

That are so dim they can no longer see
To guide the cunning pen in the fair scroll ;
Yea, by all these, and by the hope I have
That when I die, I shall not wholly die,
I swear, young King, that help is very near
If only thou endure ; therefore be hopeful.

KING.

And who, I pray thee, is to be the bearer
Of this good help thou talk'st of, and I need
So sorely ?   Where is any strong enough
And willing, who would break this iron host ?
My neighbours are all cowering for sheer dread
In what poor holes they can creep into.   None
Now have the heart to stand by me.

ELISHAMA.

Last night
I dreamed I stood upon the hill of Olives
Looking to the holy city, and I saw
Out of the midst a tree of wondrous leafage
Much like a cedar, grow, and growing spread
Broad branches out, and shadow all the city.
Then saw I a great eagle, mighty-winged,
Come with a rush that made the mountain whirl,
And snatch at the fair cedar, as it were
Some quarry ; then I saw, from out the west,
A mightier eagle swoop upon the first,
And bear him screaming earthward, till he fell

Prone, and I saw him not.   Methinks this dream
Shews surely help is coming from the west,
And fall to Salem's render, whose foul beak
Shall taste of dust, erelong.

KING.

The dream is vain.

Pharaoh has long forgotten his old bond ;
Else wherefore has he left me undefended
To bear the bitter brunt of this fierce storm ?

ELISHAMA.

Say not the dream Elishama dreamed is vain :
Time was, young King, when my great lord thy
    father
Would hearken to my word, and deem it right
To follow all Elishama had counselled ;
Let not the least of all his branches laugh
To scorn the words he honoured.   Nor has Pharaoh
Forgotten that great oath he swore with thee—
Ay, by his gods he swore't, and sealed his faith
With sacrifice—to be thy friend and helper
So long as thou wert true—mark me, so long.
And Pharaoh is no craven, though his hands
Have been of late so busy in repressing
The tumults of the South, where nimble Cush
Bites ever, dog-like, at his master's heels.
Had not his kingly father died ere he

Could follow up his victory, and smite
The men of Cush with mighty hand, and lay
The land of Cush for ever at his feet,
Hophrah of Egypt never would have left
His leaguèd friend fast in the grip of siege
And famine ; but his realm to him is dear
As thine to thee—dearer, should I not say?
And therefore is he full of anxious cares—
But not for long, I think ; soon will he come
To lay this upstart Babel low as she
Is low, the lordly Nineveh of yore.

KING.

No craven may he be, and yet his strength
Be but the ghost of the brave heart within.
Babel has countless numbers—armies here,
At Riblah with their King, and at the bound
Of Shinar to the sunrise, watching Elam ;
To say nought of the many scattered bands
Here, there, and everywhere, throughout his king-
　　dom.
What hosts can Pharaoh have to match all these,
If his whole might be busy with one war?

ELISHAMA.

They are with him are better far than numbers.
He has, in sooth, a lordly retinue ;
No mere beasts these, who when their leader falls
Turn tail, and fly off faster than they came,

But hearts that stand, each one himself a host,
Though leaderless, 'gainst overwhelming numbers ;
And fight on till they fall, thrust thro' and thro',
Nigh buried in a breastwork of dead foes.
Ay, I have seen their valour ; for I fled
When I was young as thou art young, the fury
Of that mad ancestor of thine, King Amon,
Who filled Jerusalem's streets with holy blood
And all her homes with sorrow. Mine own life
(That had but barely 'scaped Manasseh's jaws)
I knew he sought ; so flew to Mizraïm
To find a ready helper and defender
In noble-hearted Psametik, whose blood
Flows yet in Hophrah's veins. There did I see
That never-to-be-conquered band of warriors
From far-off Javan, and the ocean-isles
Of Elishah—proud of their land were they
As we of ours ; for they had come, not led
By their own will, but his who ruled them there,
Friend to the Pharaoh ; whom, as their own lord,
They loved and served ; and oftentime I saw them
And heard their speech—fair speech that flowed
    from out
Their mouths like dashing water, with a sound
Sweet as the silver horns, what time the song
Of praise arises, and the Temple fills
With music. Once with Pharaoh's host I went

In a great galley up the River, far
As the naked border of the land of Cush,
Where we found all the strength of Cush drawn out
In battle order.   Pharaoh bade this band
Charge first to break the forest of keen spears
Flashing before us ; tarrying made they none,
But with one bound they charged, and with one voice
Lift up their lofty song of war, that rolled
Like summer thunder while the keen storm fell
Of steel-shaft lightning on their foes.   Thereat
The southern host broke up like chaff before them,
Chased to the mountain clefts and sandy plains.
Back came they singing triumph, and would none
Of weighty guerdon like the others, but
Only a wreathèd diadem that Pharaoh
Had wrought for them, what time he went to war.
Full many thousands Hophrah has of these,
And these, methinks, are match enough for Babel
With all his rabble, yell they e'er so loud ;
No yelling will avail them with the spears
Of Pharaoh's islesmen at their throats.   Even now,
If visions are not vain, they come.

KING.

Well said,
And like my fearless counsellor of old !
Thou comfortest the heart in me anew.—
Farewell, my father—I will go and rest

And, maybe, sleep—and if I dream of hope
This counsel will I follow, come what will !

[*Exit.*

ELISHAMA (*alone*).

Farewell, poor weakling of a noble stock ;
But born, I fear, to drag down guiltless men
To ruin with thee ! Never art thou sure
A whole day through, of that unsteady heart
That wears the leprosy of fear far more
Than any flush of courage. Well, go sleep !
Light chance of any dream of hope from out
That craven spirit. While the dastard crew
Howl round thy walls, thou sleepest—shame on thee!
Had I young arms like thine, verily this night
Would I lead out our bravest at the foe
Whose dull hearts sleep within their brazen armour ;
Heavy with wine are they, and feasting ; prone
The most of them, and open to surprise.—
But no ; this shadow of a King commands
That no one stir out from our gates, but all
Keep close within, and hurl their coward stones
From off our rampart. Father Abraham,
That we should come to this !
                    What strange dull roar
Is that seems rolling hither from the gate ?
It sounds like thunder ; but no thunder rumbles
So near the voice of men. Haply the herd

Of Babel swine are shouting in their feast,
Wrought to mad heat with wine—or maybe strain
Throats in hoarse praises of their god.—Ay, now
It rises yet again!

GEDALIAH.

My lord and King,
I thirst to hear thy purpose, and fulfil.—
Elishama here?—Father, I pray thee pardon;
I thought to find the King——

ELISHAMA.

No, my young lord,
Here thou wilt find no King to-night, for he
Sleeps 'neath his roof in quiet—not in peace,
Nor ever will, if I have strength to stay him,
Until such time as Babel is laid low.
I know thine errand.

GEDALIAH.

What is that to thee?
'Twould better far become thy hoary hairs
To press the pillow at this hour. In sooth,
Night dews are harm to aged limbs—this mist
That steals on us so surely, is not well
For thee.

ELISHAMA.

Mock not mine age, thou shameless one!
Were't not for striplings such as thou, forever

Weakening our King with fool's words, we should be
Rid of our foes long erst.—But no foes they
To those are eager servants to their will
And work their bidding unbeknown.

GEDALIAH.

Wert thou
But younger, that one word would be thy last
And choke thee in the utterance. Now I know
Who has been here and wrought on Zedekiah
With crafty speech, and turned his feeble soul
From looking on the morning, to the cold
Grey empty west ; shame on thee for thy pains !

(Enter MESSENGER, *suddenly.)*

MESSENGER.

O woe, forever woe ! Our city's lost !
Fly, as ye love your lives, my lords, and follow
Our King to refuge from the terrible foe !

ELISHAMA.

Gasp not there, fellow ; tell thy message, plain ;—
No foe could pass our gates, except their bars
Were loosened from within.

MESSENGER.

'Tis even so.
My lord, I will speak plainly, if I can ;
But grief, and wind-swift striving through the
    streets

With my fell news, nigh choked me. 'Twas the
    people,
Who, mad for food, they said, flew on the guard
That kept our gate, and slew them ; then cried, loud
As thunder, as they shot back heavy bars
And flung the great gate open, ' Come ye in,
Ye men of Babel, all Jerusalem
Is yours, so will ye only give us food !'
And while they cried, the forefront of the foe
Poured in, and battered down remorselessly
The armless people—'twas a sickening sight
To see, that spear-struck trampled multitude—
Shouting in laughter like night-prowling dogs
Redfanged with blood new shed, 'Food wanted ye?
Ye shall have food in plenty, maybe not
The sort ye love, but harder and more cold !—
Cut them down, all !'   But when the leaders came,
And checked them, sternly bidding all beware
Of killing and of robbing—for throughout
The merchant-quarter were they spread in ravage,
Glutting their murderous maws with spoil—they fell
One by one back into their ranks again
To wait their leaders' will.   I barely 'scaped
The edge of slaughter, and came breathless on
To warn the King, who now is gone with all
His house in fleetest flight.   Ye hear them now
(God help them) picking each one stealthily

His way down yonder valley, by the gardens
Our lord delighted in in times gone by—
O woe, that he should ever so forsake them
To fly far off for life !

GEDALIAH.

Speak truly, fellow,
And say if thou know'st whither he is gone ?

MESSENGER.

To Rabbath Ammon, so they said, my lord,
Where he may find sure refuge with King Baalis,
Already shelterer of many sons
Of Judah, who have fled there since the siege.

ELISHAMA.

True, true, thou sayest ; for one rebel shoot
Of mine is there—would he were in his grave !
I stayed his hand from bloodshed often ; yet
Held him, I thought to the warrior's duty.   Vainly
I strove, for now he swells that heathen's state
And rears his violent heart up to all ill.

GEDALIAH.

So ends our valiant master.   Fare him well !
Long enough has he lived, to dig a pit
Of lasting death for fair Jerusalem,
And see her lordly turrets tottering in.
'Tis hard, Jehovah lets such cankers live
And chokes them not ere birth.—It seems, my lord,

We have not much to look for now, but death,
Or shame and sorrow, drowning deep.   Already
The end of all draws near.

ELISHAMA.

                      Talk not of shame ;
Shame came not where Elishama had breath,
And never shall.   Sorrow I have, how deep
He only knows, who high in heaven hears
And mourns for me ; and death I soon shall taste ;
No bitterness to me, who foot it faltering
On the grave's edge already, since I die
Green in the unwithered honour of my fathers
And crowned with David's fame.   When ruin falls,
As fall it must erelong, and blazing fire
Kindled by godless hands, on the fair Temple
Of Him whose servant I have ever been
And hope to be in death—if any ask
For Elishama, bid them go seek him where
The cherubim spread out their wings on glory
In days that are no more.   When thickest flames
Beat on them, and they shed their golden wings
To earth, and are not, haply from my ashes
A steam of goodly savour shall arise
Even to Jehovah's throne.—Is that I hear
The tread of armèd men ?   Now by the blood
Of holy David, coursing in my veins,
I will not tarry here, to meet foul scorn

And foulest hands of heathen laid on me,
Who am as spotless as a lamb decked out
For the great sacrifice—I will not stay !
Not out of consecrated ground and walls
Will I die, but once in Jehovah's Temple,
Their brutish rage may vent itself on me
And on my Temple too. The glory gone,
What need of empty carcass wherein once
It dwelt, and dwelling lighted all the world?
Yet, some faint trace of power may linger there,
As lingers sweetest odour in the cup
That once held precious wine. My fair young lord,
I leave thee to thy friends—and the glad thought
Of safety bought by treason. Fare thee well !

[*Exit.*

GEDALIAH.

There was the old lion speaking still, through age
That shook his roar, and in the face of death !
Spite of his stubborn heart, by mine own soul
I honour him, and wish him glorious end ;—
For if aright I know him, nought will he
Of captive bonds—death rather, swiftest death ;—
In that I wish him death, I wish no ill ;
He has lived too long already—long enough
To drag destruction down on us by braving
Such as fair words would gain. Yet, since his heart
Was upright, and no evil harboured there,

Glory, as in his life, be in his death !—
Meseems that even I am not exempt
From stroke of slaughter, while deep darkness holds
Unknown to one another friend and foe ;
'Twere well to seek the captains, ere some band
Fall on my life.—Ah, who is this, that comes
In flowing raiment, and a blaze of gems
That glow i' th' torch flame like a heaven of stars
This inky night ?   His face seems one that I
Have seen before—but where ?

(*Enter* NERGAL SHAREZER *with Soldiers.*)

NERGAL SHAREZER.

     What brings thee here,
Thou man of Judah ?—Old Ahikam's son,
Or else these brands but mock me——

GEDALIAH.

     In good sooth,
My lord, I am the same—young Gedaliah ;
My father was Ahikam, who is dead.

NERGAL SHAREZER.

Ay, now I mind me how we met—long past.
Right glad am I, to find mine olden friend
Ere harm was wrought on him.

GEDALIAH.

     How merit I
My lord's great goodwill so ?

NERGAL SHAREZER.

                Do ye stand back.—
Now to our friendly tale.—Rememberest not
Those many kindnesses I had of thee
When, years ago, I came on royal errand
Hither, and found warm shelter 'neath thy roof?
I mind me then thy father was alive—
Kindly old man and righteous, was Ahikam—
Who gave me courtliest welcome, bade me eat
And drink, of all his best ; and a fair bed
Was spread for me, the fairest that he had ;
The while his stripling Gedaliah strove
To cheer my soul with softest speech, and songs—
Sweeter to me than all the songs of Babel
Sung from of old, or what of later days
Hired bards may weave to win their master's smile
Or scattered purse, or seat at feasting board ;
I love them not; with weary heart I hear them ;
Hoarse as they are with names of numbrous gods
And reeking with their praises,—sweet as those
I heard in my fair childhood 'mong the hills
Of Media—herdsmen sang them in night hours
To while their watch away.—Boy wert thou then,
Yet manhood hath not changed thee in my eyes.

GEDALIAH.

Now God be praised, who watcheth evermore
On us, like loving father on his sons !—

My lord, I little counted on such fall
Of great good fortune on me, as has brought
So noble a deliverer.   What poor service
I did thee in years past was but the due
To every stranger (so our fathers teach us),
And not done, brings us shame and foul reproach.
'Tis strange, to praise our songs—thou art no son
Of Babel or the plains.

NERGAL SHAREZER.

                              No, thanks to Him
Whose sacred flame will rise on us to-morrow,
No worshipper am I of wood and stone,
And hate their slavish praises.   If my will
Hold good for aught with the great King, this city
And her high Temple crown, shall feel no touch
Of violating hands—nor shall true priest
Or faithful prophet lose one drop of blood.
Our lord is no mere torturer—though stern
To such as wrong him, he will never push
His anger to the bitter end, but ever
Yields graciously to them that sue him right.
He loves not war ; the battle crash to him
Is hateful ; he would have no enemies ;
But when one shakes the corner of his power
He turns on him perforce.   If that blind King
Of thine had meddled not with Pharaoh, still
His throne had stood on peace.   The rule of aught

The west encircles must of nature fall
To one of two, King Hophrah or our lord ; .
If Hophrah gain it, then the realm of Babel
Trembles from end to end ; but if with us
The lordship stay, our master's seat is sure,
And having peace on one side, he is free
To centre all his strength (with due allowance
For guard of sunward borders) on his purpose,
Whereon his soul is set, of rearing up
Rich palace-roofs, and temples at whose glory
His fathers would turn pale.—The day when he
Set forth on this emprise, nigh two years gone,
I rode with him down our broad way, betwixt
Its soaring buildings, toward the bridge that leads
Borsippa-ward.   A gloom was in his eyes,
And he said mournfully, as we sped on
Past thronging packs of people gathered there
To shout their lord fair fortune in the fight,
' How know I if I now cast latest looks
On this my handiwork, unfinished yet ?
Maybe ; then who is there of all my children
Heir to his father's spirit with his crown ?
If I return not, may not this my city,
Pride of my heart of hearts, be in her flush
Of maiden beauty sent the reeling path
That shelves sheer down to ruin ?   Bel forbid !
Would peace were in my borders at this hour.'

With that he sighed a heavy sigh, and never
Spake of these things again.　But oftentime
I have seen him sad and silent, and bethought me
Of those his parting words, and known full well
How his heart yearns for peaceful home-return
And a glad people's cries.—

　　　　　　　　Now, since thy father
(On whose fair memory rest unending peace)
Is past all taste of earthly honour, thou,
Firstfruit of his begetting, for his sake
And for thine own, inheritest all good
I would have striven to gain him from our master,
Governorship of Judah ; if my toil
At kingly ears bear fruit, Ahikam's son
Shall lord it so, and triumph on his foes,
Glad servants then of him they mocked before.

GEDALIAH.

My loving lord, thou read'st my dearest wish ;—
Not that I would have wronged my king, if only
His heart had learned submission, bent to law ;
But when I knew all lost, and he—O shame !—
In coward flight, meseemed that very well
'Twould be, could I, who ever sought and strove
To make his peace with Babel, gain some power
To cheer my brethren's lot, so starred with ill.
If, as I deem, some influence with the king
Is thine—

NERGAL SHAREZER.

      He leans upon me, calls me friend;
Sets by his side at table, honours me
Beyond all other lords of his. Doubt not
My voice with him is able to gain this;
Ere many days are past, be fortune fair,
All, as we wish, shall be.

(*Enter* SOLDIERS *with the* WARDER *prisoner; one
speaks.*)

SOLDIER.

             An't please my lord,
We found this man lurking behind a bastion;
He moved not when we challenged him, and when
We seized him, struggled not; yet kept his eye
Fixed on us, as a man does in a trance.
I pray my lord we kill him, for he seems
Possessed of some ill demon, who mayhap
Will urge him to fall on us presently.
We are all one in this.

GEDALIAH.

          My lord, this man,
When our King's father was a child, took on him
That faithful service, which through every change
And storm of fortune, he fulfilled till now;
Grey has he grown, and weatherbeaten, watching
For Salem's safety, from this very wall.

Let his dry leaf be left to dangle yet
A little longer, from the tree of life ;
Count me his pledge and bond.

NERGAL SHAREZER.

Men, touch him not.
Let him go where he will, and pass this word
Through all your ranks. No murmuring, quick,
    be off !—

GEDALIAH.

I thank thee from my soul for this good turn ;
Dear is this man, and reverend, to us all.
He knew my grandsire Shaphan, and old Amon,
Josiah's father, served, albeit he got
Small thanks therefore from that stern slaughterer ;
And many tales he knows of the old times,
Dread stories of those mighty ones that held
The land, what time our fathers swarmed across
From Moab, such long lengths of years ago ;
And how lord David lurked in hiding-holes
For fear of Saul, and darted out in raids
Of desperate valour, winning sometimes spoil
And sometimes a fair wife. Then he would tell
How, in the years gone by, the hosts of Asshur
Came crashing on the land, in multitude
Untold as thronging locusts, when they come
From the hot South, devouring fruit and leaf,

And pay back tears and famine. 'O the woe
They wrought, those men of Asshur,' he would say,
'Judah they seared like fire, and furthermore
Left bitterness in Israel's cup for ever.'
Talker he was, yet not upon his lips
But in his bosom's depth, he kept his heart,
Tear-quick for other's sorrow, alway. Years
May he live yet, I hope, to serve me well
As he has served his kingly lords before.
Again I give thee grateful thanks ——

NERGAL SHAREZER.

Not so ;
Now are we brothers, and the will of one
Becomes the other's deed.—Say, who is this
That with wild eyes and raven hair outstreaming
Floats towards us like some shadow—none of earth ?
See it comes nearer, nearer——

GEDALIAH.

Hush, my lord ;
The prophetess !

NAOMI.

Aye, I have found ye now.
Quake not, and turn so craven pale, lord Nergal,
But hearken to my word ; and he that shrinks
Shivering behind thee, traitor, whose foul name
I know too well, shall listen. Jehovah saith :
'Albeit I sorely laid My hand on Judah

In just requital for the sin she sinned,
Forsaking My due praise and sacrifice
To worship graven blocks of senseless stone,
Not alway will I punish, and moreover
Their heathen hands I wrought My judgment by
Shall not laugh Me to scorn ; but I will side
With Mine own people, when they purge their hearts
In pure repentance, as I sided when
High-hearted Deborah and doubting Barak
With half a score of thousands at their feet,
Followed Me to the battle, broke the hosts
Of Jabin, when that brawling ancient water
Of Kishon reddened with his bravest blood
And swept his captain's corpses to the sea ;
Fought I not then for Israel ? Sang he not
The triumph-song? So shall he sing once more.
Say, Naomi, Jehovah's wrath is wakened,
And it is coming, coming ; all the havoc
Ye Chaldees work on this My dwelling-place
Shall fall on Babel, hundredfold and soon.
Think not that I, with idle hand in bosom,
Will see this garden of My earth betrod
With trampling hoofs to death, and unavenged ;
Tremble, ye men of Babel, for the days
Of woe and bitter wailing overhang
Your heads even now—weep and repent, before
The hour is past—bring ye meet sacrifice

To this High Place where I have set My Name ;
So 'scape your brethren's wrath, and save your souls
Alive.'
   Thus saith Jehovah—heed it, ye.—
Moreover in His visions have I been
But yesternight—mark ye what I beheld.
Turn not away, lord Nergal—'tis a thing
That touches thee too closely ; stay and hear.—
Meseemed at first I wandered in dark ways
And found no path—when suddenly I saw
A line of light like lightning leap across
The great north heaven—broader and broader grew
The rift, with ragged edges rolling over
Like a fire-shrivelled scroll ; the while there fell
A flood of thunder on me, where I stood
Full of amaze and fear—who on the wings
Of that dread roar seemed rising, as a cloud,
And felt no more, but was, and saw, and heard.
Now was all heaven one blaze of golden light,
When with a clang of trumpets terrible
Came forth supreme Jehovah, chariot-borne
As for the war. His shield was fringed with fire,
And in His hand the slaying lightning trembled
Athirst for death ; four horses spreading wings
That whirred high over thunder, drew Him on,
Who strode within a car of sapphire crystal
Wheeling on flashing flame, that hurtled down

The steep of heaven right royally.   Far above
Rose rank past rank o' th' Mighty, weaponed all
To the full, and breathing from their eyes fierce
    longing ;
Rank beyond rank below, sworded and speared
And bearing ruby shields before them, swept
Down thundering paths amain, while trumpeters
Shrilled out for onset, all that countless throng
Shouting the battle-cry in exultation ;—
Then saw I far below them, in the dew
Of sleep yet wrapt, proud towered Babel lie,
Bathed in their light like morning.   Peak and roof
And battlement, edged red with living gold
Shone out to meet their onset—whereupon
Rose up a sullen mutter from the Deep,
And forth from foulest darkness came all gods
That boast of Chaldee worship, Chaldee praise ;
Like smoke they struggled up, gathering their hosts
To battle as they came.   Then with a roar
Like mightiest waters, clothed in mist that breathed
The shafted death, fell on them all that flood
Of Lord Jehovah's war—nought did I see,
But felt the air I hung in thrill and quiver
When both their vanguards met—and when the
    smoke
Of dreadful battle rolled away, I saw
Those false gods failing underneath the brunt

Of angel-falchions shooting into Night.—
Bright Bel I saw, his golden hair all dabbled
With life-blood newly shed, go flaming down
Where black gulfs yawned below him—Nebo saw
Hurled from his temple-home in loved Borsippa,
Clay-cake and graver clenched in dying hands—
Rimmon came thunderous, striding cloud, and sped
Straight at Jehovah's chariot wheels, when fire
Flew round him clinging—cloud and rider both
Passed like a mist away and were no more—
Voluptuous Ishtar, crownless, whelmed in shame
And deathly pale, fell shrieking—and the Seven,
The sexless ones who dwell in deepest deeps,
Wreaking all ill on mortals—spitting now
Their venom-spite at their own kindred, ranged
Them on Jehovah's side—to be swift sped
To death with whistling clamour, ghostly shrill ;
And all their hosts came showering down upon them,
Howling in lamentation as they fell.
Then on the sleeping city——

NERGAL SHAREZAR.

Peace, oh peace !

Maid, I adjure thee by the God thou servest,
By thine own honour, and thy father's graves,
Spare me and cease—have mercy——

NAOMI.

Sword and fire

And all the hoarded might of strong destruction
Wielded by heavenly hands, came raining fast—
Oh joy! blood-red with wrath the firmament
Looked frowning down—even now I hear once more
That splitting shout of victory, that swoop
Of sword-flames, starting up the cityful
From sleep to swiftest death—I hear the groan
Dull and half-smothered, of the godless ones!—
Jehovah called Euphrates then.   Heaven-high
The river rose, roaring, and shook his mane
Of waters, like an angry beast—then bowing
His blue neck, overarching Babel, fell;
And through the crash of toppling roofs shot up
The shriek of women, one keen cry; then all
Was still.   I swooned away for very gladness,
Or seemed to swoon, and woke; yet in awaking
There came across my ears a sound much like
The gurgling wash of waters, far below;
I minded me of Babel's fall, and smiled.

False sprout of Shaphan, whom that grey-beard
      prophet
Lures at his empty bidding on to death,
Hearken, I say—beware, the high-set seat
Bodes ill to thee;—why should I wish thee well?
Go, quick, and take it!   Chaldee, guide the blind;
Lead to the cliff's edge, bid him dance for joy,
Then watch thy dear friend diving deep and deeper

Into such gloom thou'd shrink to follow him to!
Try this same footing after, if thy heart
Incline thee.   Sharpest curse of all the curses
Have ye of me for farewell!

[*Exit Naomi.*

GEDALIAH.
O my brother,
It is a terrible thing, when God so looks
Out at the wild eyes threatening—and such ill
As my heart dies to think on.   Knew I only
She spoke vain words, and not the baulkless purpose,
Then might I rest in peace.

NERGAL SHAREZER.
Fie on thee, faint-heart ;
Let not a woman's raving shake thee so ;—
Who is this maid, now tell me—she is gone,
No need for fear—yet, when she turned far off
To look on us, how her eyes glittered blue
Athwart the darkness, keen as winter stars !—
We can breathe freer now.

GEDALIAH.
If ever life
Was charged with bitterness from end to end,
I think 'twas hers—scarce from her mother's breast
She felt the tooth of sorrow rankle deep
In her young heart—her father slain in fight

Against the Chaldee, making stand for Salem,
And with her weary mother she must foot
That rending road to Babel far away ;
Mixed with the thronging heap of sorrow urged
On faltering feet, what time Jehoiachin
Was swept off to captivity, and Salem
Bled of her best and bravest, twelve years gone ;
Soon died the mother, torn from clinging arms
To grace some Chaldee chieftain's luxury,
And wild-eyed lonely Naomi, left the sport
Of burning blasts of hate and gusts that freeze
Of icy scorn, wore out some wretched years
And grew up strange and silent, shunning sound
And sight of man.   When twice seven years had set
Their seal upon her beauty, and her bud
Of childhood blossomed to a pale rose bloom,
Some lustful lord of Babel—so they say—
Cast on her fair sad face his swinish eyes
And sought to bear her off—but ere the slaves
Could do their master's bidding, she was gone.
None found her ever after in those walls,
But some few months ago, we saw her here
As now we saw her, wandering unbeknown
And uttering strangest wisdom and wild speech ;
And it was told how she had found a shelter
With merchants of Arabia, in whose train
She followed far as Riblah, and thence found—

By what wild toil I know not—way unhindered
Hither.   And now 'tis rumoured marvellous visions
Not unsent of Jehovah—may He grant
'Tis not so, but vain dreaming—haunt her ever ;
And truly wondrous light looks through her eyes,
And in her speech, my heart keeps telling me,
There sounds a voice that bodes me bitter bale.

NERGAL SHAREZER.

Cheer thee, my friend ; take not such heed of words
Fallen from a witless tongue.   But what a draught
Of gall i' th' cup of life, for childish lips
To drain to the bitter bottom !   By the sun,
My master's warriors work much ill in Judah ;
Would they were home again, and hands blood-
  stained
But now, were only harvesting in peace
The corn, our yellow sea, that heaves and rolls
Waiting the reapers' toil, and fares but ill
In servant hands, when masters are away ;
Then might this strife-scorched land of thine rejoice
In peace and plenteous seasons, bursting barns,
And gather all her warworn stricken children
To her broad bosom motherlike, and breathe
Into their hearts the balm of happy days ;
Then would thy brethren bless their fair young lord
And bring him summer fruits, and all due homage,
And prosper, they and he.

GEDALIAH.

       I cannot speak,
My lord and brother, the rich gratitude
That wells up from my soul to meet such love ;
It takes away all utterance.

     (*Enter a* SOLDIER.)

    SOLDIER.

       Good my lord,
I have foul news to tell.

    NERGAL SHAREZER.

      What news ? what news ?

    SOLDIER.

Spite of my lord's command that none should lay
Sword or any violent hands on any Hebrew,
The white-haired priest, the scribe——

    NERGAL SHAREZER.

       What sayest thou ?
Dared any slave of mine so scorn my orders ?

    SOLDIER.

One of our army followed him within
The temple doors, and slew him, as he stood
With outspread palms praying before the altar
Of incense, so it seems—he took his spear
And smote between his shoulders, and he fell
Right on the altar, heart-blood flowing out
And mingling with hot incense. So he died.
Lord Sarsechim seized the man, and has him fast

In ward for his ill deed—who sped me here
With earnest supplication for thy counsel
In this, and weightier matters.

NERGAL SHAREZER.

Say, I come.—
[*Exit* SOLDIER.

Brother of Judah, if it should so hap
That any lay a forcing hand upon thee,
Remember that my name is powerful
To give free passage anyway, from here
To Riblah.   Furthermore, this signet ring
Will bring who wears it even to the throne
Whereupon he that lords this land now sits,
Nebuchadnezzar, king of kings on earth.
Take it, and use if need be.   Fare thee well.

[*Exit* NERGAL SHAREZER.

GEDALIAH.

And now at last my dearest dream draws near
Its high fulfilment, and this lovely land,
Soil of my fathers, sown with bones of glory,
Nigh mine, for joy or sorrow.   Stumbling-stone
Is none—the bravest, bitterest foe I had
Slumbers on holy ground.   That he sleep on
In peace, I grudge him not.   All hindrance sped
(For after Elishama no living soul
In Judah durst oppose his will to mine),
What else but triumph spread before—what else

But seas of joy for Judah and for me?
That lion's grandwhelp Ishmael lives, 'tis true,
Bears me a hate not less—but why fear him,
Crouched in the tent of Ammon?—Ah, to Baalis
Methought the slave said King and all his guard
Were gone—what if it were a cloak to blind
Our eyes withal, who rise when he is set,
Yet until then are pale—not lights to guide
And cheer, but phantom butts of scorn!—Ah, fool,
Fool that I was to revel in rich dreams
Of might and glory, while a King yet lives
Who meditates mayhap a suppliant suit
To him of Babel—which if once he gain,
Confusion to our hopes! This plan of ours
Might never leak out, yet I know no love
Burns in his heart of hearts to me. Too soon,
Fool-like, too soon, I reckoned, ere the way
Was clear before me; if Josiah's seed
Reach Riblah and gain the Chaldee, all is lost.

(*Enter a* MESSENGER.)

MESSENGER.

Sore news I bring, my lord, sore news and foul;
The King is taken, and as good as dead,
And all his captains and his chosen ones
Winnowed away like chaff before some gust
When winds are out in summer—but the wheat,
The chosen corn, the fair wheat and the holy,

Become the prey of spoilers—woe is me !
The Chaldees took him in the hills, just through
The pass they call Adummim, half-way down
To Jericho ; where robbers oftentime
Have fallen upon our camels, smote and spoiled
And wrought our city merchants mickle woe ;—
There burst on him that cloud of clanging arms
Poured down in thousands from each rock and cave
And yawning of the mountains, as they trod
Their weary way beside the torrent-brink
Roaring not now with waters, dry and dead ;
Fiercely they fought and long, the King not least,
Till strength was spent, and sword and spear were
      broken,
While for each foe they slaughtered, nigh a score
Came flooding down upon them in their stead ;—
When the King saw his young men mostly fallen
Or flying fast before strange spears, he bowed
His gracious neck to earth and made his moan,
(The while the ring of wolfish eyes crept closer)
Crying ' Jehovah, hast Thou now no help
For Thine anointed King? That crown Thou gavest,
Suffer not unclean hands to rend from me ;
Darken their eyes in their presumption, so
They find me not, forsaken as I am.'
But while his lips yet moved, they swooped on him,
Bound fast, and speedily gat him off, away—

Where, I know not—myself was left for dead
Among his slain ones, and fetched back such life
By stress of gasping, as has sped me here
To tell my woefullest of all ill tales.

GEDALIAH.

This is strange news, and sudden. We must go
To the Temple court together, where the chiefs
Of Judah, and some other, sit in council
Resolving our affairs. Rouse thee and come ;
Thou shalt be tended quickly, and rewarded—
Ay, to thy heart's desire. (*Aside.*) Now do I breathe
New life !

[*Exeunt* GEDALIAH *and* MESSENGER.

WARDER.

So ran the ancient oracles.
The prophets fell, whose blood flew up to heaven
Shrieking for righteous vengeance, long ago ;
The house of David slew them, and upon
The head of David's seed a fateful doom
Hung hovering—even all the great glad time
God-loved Josiah held just royalty,
But yet, with all his goodness, could not ward
The death-stroke off, that fell when he was gone.
A bitter fall !—But fairer days, though few,
From time to time were ours, and foolishly
Judah grew quite forgetful, laughed and sang
In light contentment, like a wanton child

Upon a pitfall's edge. Too foolish ye
To dream the eternal oracles could slumber !—
Yet so it was ; but righteousness could save,
And purging off that curse of wizard charms
That brings our great curse downward ! Nevermore
Will ye, the captives of to-morrow, come
And nest you in your mountains as of old ;
Or if ye do, 'twill only be when lords
Are weary of the hands that yield them toil,
Or powerless, by some fell calamity,
To keep their bond no longer. Be it so,
By high Jehovah, and the Mighty, all !
Yet 'tis too far for hope. But if it come,
Rebellious Judah will have learnt too dearly
What a high shield they slank from, when the witch,
And star-watcher, and guesser by the rods,
Lured them from that clear glory wont to fill
The sacred space, and dazzle holy eyes ;
And gave but wind in recompense ! Methinks
If that day dawn, ye will be wiser then ;
But what a dear-bought wisdom, to lose all
Ye hold most good, and leave your many bones
Of old forefathers whitening where the land
Bred dumb despair and thraldom !

                               Nevermore,
Oh David, wilt thou sweep through fairest halls
With kingly robe around thee, and with blare

Of trumpets, clang of cymbals, song of slaves ;
No more will that light soul, like thistledown
Dance on each wave of faction fresh up-puffed
By breath of flatterers fawning ; good and ill
Both dead for thee—unless (our God forbid)
Thou, wretched one, hast 'scaped death, but not
    shame
Far bitterer—the spurn of scorn, the jeer
Of insolent hate—the blighting name of slave !
I pray Thee, Lord Jehovah—for I feel
Thee still our God, our fostering Father still,
Whatso black deeps we wade in—send on him
A saving boon of death betime, so he
Drain not that withering poison, a slave's life ;
Let not the last light twig of David's tree
Die decking heathen pride.—

                False, flaunting dawn,
Why rises it in rosy robes and gold
To laugh the grey night out of countenance ?
Peace, wanton, hide that mocking smile of thine,
And bid the sun, thy doting lover, tarry
Awhile with thee below the hills ; so leave
The sons of sorrow in a seemly gloom
To taste their heritage !

              Still it uplifts
Those flashing curtains for the paramour
Who peeps with fiery eye from the green fringe

Of Olivet, and turns dim leaves to gold ;
A fire about the roots of sentinel pines
That keep watch over Jordan—burning now
Even as he did when came glad tidings, lighting
A blaze of triumph, flung from heart to heart
And spreading seawide o'er Jerusalem—
That Nineveh, the Pitiless—our scourge
And hammer of all the nations—split and shattered
Lay at her hater's mercy.   Then we blessed
That golden lamp of heaven, that beamed on us
As though he shared our glee.   Far other hour
Rolls on us now the mocking morning's smile,
When she, with ashen garments rent in storm
And gusts of clamorous lamentation ever
Bearing big tears to earth, should look on all
This sorrow.—Now meseems it well to go
Unheard and unbeheld, right out away
From sick Jerusalem, and stretch spent limbs
In darkness—rid of this blue mockery
Of day, this dancing leering ball of fire—
In darkness, which is very peace, to die.   [*Exit.*

Ψυχὴ γὰρ εὔνους καὶ φρονοῦσα τοὔνδικον
Κρείσσων σοφιστοῦ παντός ἐστιν εὑρέτις.

SOPHOKLES.

Metod callum weold
Gumena cynnes,
Swá he nú git déth ;
Forthan bith andgit
Æghwær sélest,
Ferhthes forethanc :
Fela sceal gebídan
Leófes and láthes,
Se the longe her
On thyssum win-dagum
Worulde brúceth.   .   .
Ure æghwylc sceal
Ende gebídan
Worulde lífes :
Wyrce se the móte
Dómas ær deáthe ; ¹
Thæt bith driht-guman
Unlífgendum
Æfter sélest.

BEOWULF.

SONGS OF THE WAYSIDE.

I.

WATCH ! for the night is past, its shadows flee,
While, azure as the eyes of infancy,
   Rises the morning with one hopeful star
To guide us yet awhile on life's loud sea.

Hold we our way right on, nor suffer aught
Of fear or of foreboding in our thought ;
   The way is clear, and day is near, and we
Bring the same heart of hope we ever brought.

Only beware we, while the dawn before
Our bounding prow swells brighter evermore,
   Lest at the lulling of a Siren song,
Our hands grow listless, and let fall the oar.

And though unwonted storms around us rave,
With hearts undaunted all their fury brave,
   Bending our eyes upon that beacon-star
That flashes far and fearless on the wave.

So, when the mists of morning 'gin to pale
Before the breathing of a balmier gale,
   That orient roseflush fall on us unscathed,
Loosing the folds forth of an unrent sail.

And when the unruffled royal harbour we
Enter, at length from storms and surges free,
   Haply our bark, if steadfast hands have steered,
Will bear us after on a sunnier sea.

What says the holy sage, Mark Antonine,
Brightest and best of all the sceptred line,
   Who fostered Virtue to her perfect flower,
And well-nigh linked our human with divine ?

' Live not as though thou looked to live for years
Unnumbered—even now the Must-be nears ;
   While life is thine, while yet 'tis in thy might,
Let each day find thee nobler than its peers ;

' Be ever mindful, 'mid the whirl of sense,
Of thine own inmost soul's omnipotence ;
   Let all thy powers like willing slaves obey
The mystic Might that bears thee hither and hence.'

So, while we wend across the tide of time,
Shall from our lonely toiling spring a chime
   Of sweetest music, as the fateful hand
Smites sternly on our spirit's strings sublime.

For never laurel of the conqueror
Won as green guerdon of triumphant war,
   But withered with the weary brow it bound,
But sank with it in dust for evermore.

But they, the Heroes, who have bled and borne
The loftier conflict, and the crown of thorn,
   And poured their rich life's perfume for all-heal—
Crowned are with wreaths no conqueror has worn ;

The whole world's wonder, and its burning love,
Kindling upon their footsteps as they move,
   And blessings breathed of lowlier lips that yearn
Wistfully on their far fair path above.

For well we know, that out of suffering
A great and marvellous grace may often spring,
   Flowering not only for the world beside,
But even for that heart its birth-throes wring.

What if 'twere sooth, as in a saddened hour
Sang Shakspeare, 'how that life was but a flower
   In the spring time ;' if all great Nature's toils
Bore but one bloom to deck a fading bower ?

The mirage of a rainbow mist that's spread
Athwart a soundless ocean, dark and dead—
    Can this be being, and our little life
Be rounded with a sleep?   So Shakspeare said.

May not we be the sleepers, who lie here,
Slaves of each flattering hope and phantom fear,
    Coiled in the nightmare chain, Necessity,
That ever, as we shun it, seems more near ;

And this transcendent canopy of blue,
Fleece-flecked, that one white star is quivering
        through,
    And all the blossoms of the day's pure prime,
Springing to greet us through their glory of dew ;

The song of morning birds, and all the mirth
Our mother or foster mother, kindly Earth,
    Murmurs around us when we list to hear,
Gives as her best of bounty from our birth ;—

All this our being that so steadfast seems,
Be but the trembling tissue of our dreams,
    Gold-shot or sable, as the lot befall,
Cloud-bound, or glowing glorious in Love's beams?

If it be so, is not the Dreamer then
Sole sovereign of that fair world of his ken,
    Wherein he wanders, as its Archimage,
Wielding at will the eternal Where and When ?

'Tis his, who holds this fairy land in fee,
A heaven of light and love to make it be;
   Or if in evil hour he will, to shape
One scathing hateful hell of earth and sea.

Whether we toil across a tide of years,
Moaned round with wild winds drenched in human
    tears,
   Yet sometime breathing in the balmier air
As high in heaven our sun of Love appears;

Or suffer all in dream as sleepers do,
That deem what thing they seek or shun is true,
   Till, waking, starless Midnight meet their eyes,
Or sorrow melt in Morn's immortal blue ;—

The end is one, whether we dream or are ;
The world's work, which is ours, to make or mar ;
   To be and kindle suns of quenchless light,
Or stoop to darkness as a falling star.

Humanity, unchangeable, eterne,
Proud peak whereto all Nature's lowlands yearn,
   Of all the measure, and the Measurer—
Can such for ever cease to breathe and burn ?

Owning, as sun of every age and clime,
High in its own pure ether throned sublime,
   The everlasting heirdom of the ages,
The generations far beyond all time ?

A boundless spirit bounded for a day
In close-confining walls of common clay,
  That beats for ever at its bars, and yet
Half shrinks from soaring when the wall's away ;

Like butterflies that tremblingly forsake
The shelter of their sheathings when they break,
  Though breath of Summer lift their wings, and
    light
Of Summer flood the world whereto they wake ;

And yet we doubt, and double with our doubt
The films which blind our eyes to all without,
  That ring of circling foes forevermore
Drawn balefully our dim-seen path about.

Though sometime stumbling, still shall we aspire ;
The evening star that flashed through sunset's fire
  To die in darkness, if our gaze be true
Will rise the morning star of our desire.

What if the morrow swell so high before ;
Each towering billow may, if all the more
  We, like strong swimmers, breast the tide of time,
Give nearer glimpses of the wished-for shore ?

O that we even as we wish, could *know* !
Thought but adventures far as it may go,
  And leaves us on a dizzy cliff-edge, whence
We see the boundless whirl of waves below ;

Wild with white wrath the ocean wreaks its will,—
Whercover bitter winds are whistling shrill,
   And all the roaring brink of earth and sea
Foams like the floodway of some mighty mill.

Yet, through the pauses of the thundering gale,
A sound, that seems half whisper and half wail,
   Is wafted toward us as we listen above ;
' Pity and Love may pass where Thought will fail.'

And as we hail the omen, and once more
Wend our way down that steep to Life's dim shore,
   Swells yet one echo of the infinite sea—
' Pity and Love beyond all Thought can soar.'

Wherefore should shame and sorrow follow sin,
If it be not the lordly voice within
   Clanging, like some high-hung cathedral bell,
Death-dirges on the corpse they carry in ?

Desire and pride and passion overwon,
Or some dear race of duty meetly run,
   Shall not the bell chime out, in joy-notes now,
Pealing a blissful bridal new begun ?

Springs the Life-stream from heights unseen, untrod,
Where Being's source drinks in the dews of God ;
   In sight awhile, as rill and river, rolls,
Lingeringly lipping many a flowery sod ;

Until the far-off, dark, mysterious sea
Whose sighing waves we hear, yet cannot see,
    Welcome the weary waters, and erelong
To their own heavenly birthright yield them free.

Life ! is it but a sparrow's flight within
A hall where feast in winter king and kin,
    That, glad a moment in the firelight, glides
Thereout once more to the outer dark and din ?

Or may it be the wild unweeting flight
Of tropic bird caught in some cavern's night,
    That bruised and baffled in the dark awhile,
Yet finds its way through gloom from light to light?

II.

This morning Summer brooded on the sea ;
The sky above was blue as sky could be,
    And sunlit billows falling at our feet
Sang of their coral isles in slumberous glee.

But now all heaven is swathed in sullen gloom,
And leaden cloudbanks far to seaward loom,
    While under winds that whirl the withering sleet
Ocean upgathers all his solemn boom.—

Up! though the storms of winter wrestle yet,
And troubled seas below in fury fret,
   Let us not blindly in the warring days
The coming truce of God for once forget;

Carols the redbreast clearlier morn by morn,
White burgeons break upon the awakening thorn,
   And in the grass, and on each hedgerow side,
Delicate daisies one by one are born;

Soon will the swallow come from oversea,
Soon will all thickets ring with melody,
   And Earth, upspringing from her winter sleep,
Burst into beauty on each herb and tree.

Were't not for winter, who would thrill beneath
The kisses of the Spring's caressing breath,
   Or long for that deep heaven of her eyes,
The pledge of Life's day dawning out of Death?

For ever, since the old world's heart began
To pulsate with her richest life-blood, man,
   Rose the Spring-time as harbinger of hope
And loosing of long winter's bitter ban;

For Life knew not herself, in those old days,
Before the birth of Thought upon the maze,
   And Spring and Summer, Fall and Winter, flashed
To being in the light of human rays.

And so for us, if we have skill to bring
Sweet out of bitter, and make sorrow sing,
    Gilding the dusk that gathers with our glow—
Will break and blossom one immortal Spring.

Even as the holy Mother of old song,
Reft of her dear delight the winter long,
    Sprang to glad greeting 'mid the Lenten flowers,
Forgetting all the sorrow and the wrong.

Mild Mother, dewing with thy tender rain
Thy boundless brood of root and leaf and grain,
    Till they are thriven on thy bosom's breadth,
And clothe them in their glad green life again ;

We greet thy gracious presence, and we know
That whatsoever dust be hid below,
    Nameless or noble, might of thine may make
Beautiful roseblooms on that earth to blow ;

Till what seemed dust of darkness and despair,
Transfigured into a creation fair,
    Awakes to win the whole world to its love,
And with its fragrance fill the whole earth's air.

So might we, Mother, while the day is ours,
Shape in our formless sorrow as it lowers
    Some bow of promise for a brother's eye,
Some beauty blooming unto unborn hours.

Unending murmur of the sleepless sea,
What is the burden that thou sing'st to me,
   Wert ever singing from thy being's birth,
And yet shall sing in all the years to be?

Thou ever changeless in a changing earth,
The wonders thou hast witnessed from thy birth,
   Had we the wit to spell their secret out,
No wisdom were for us of better worth.

Time was, when rolling round the molten world,
A veil of clouded vapour thou wert hurled,
   Lit under by the lurid lava-glow,
Above in many a billowy mountain curled ;

Yet through all clashing conflict, and the throes
Of earth, whence rock-hewn continents arose,
   Thou ever swelled and sank, and changeless saw
Earth's summer noontides and her winter snows.

The endless round of being and of breath,
The loftier life that springs from lowlier death
   In fish and reptile, bird and beast and man—
Is this thy song, O Sea that murmureth ?

Who is to spell the secret ? Who can say
Whether the world has flung her youth away,
   Or, ever mounting with each morning's sun,
Life presses on to a diviner day ?

So may each woe, each seeming-wasted life,
Become an unseen factor in the strife,
   And lives in Earth's far future sweeter be
For all the bitter wherein ours are rife.

The wild thyme blooms, and never shows its worth,
Couching so lowly in its meadow earth ;
   But when its life is trampled by rude feet,
The soul of all its beauty springs to birth.

The winds are well-nigh sleeping ; overhead
A wintry moon, with half her splendour spread,
   Amid a ringing glory sits, and showers
Her light upon the living and the dead ;

The eye of night, that shrined in heaven's clear height
Fires with her beaming glance this brooklet bright
   Down-dancing to the yellow moonlit sea,
Till every ripple leaps in living light.

Yet other moons shall hang in heaven, and pour
Their light, when you and I shall be no more,
   Shall flash in dew-blooms and in love-lit eyes
With all their glory of the years of yore ;

So, as the years roll on, the ages roll,
Nor you nor I shall be, for mirth or dole ;
   But fall like raindrops in the stormless sea,
And sink our sundered being in the Whole.

We feel, that whatsoe'er of good be wrought
In deed or word, in suffering or in thought,
    Is not an aimless working, but a pulse
Of one great soul that throbs in All and Aught.

The Good? how shall we gauge it? one will say;
Since unlike natures unlike laws obey,
    And some hold good what others deem but ill,
Their aims as wide asunder as Night and Day?

Varies the goal of striving but in name;
Man's end were one, from whatso point he came;
    His Good abides as Heaven invariable—
Sunlit or starlit, evermore the same.

And that best Good whereafter all men yearn,
Whereto in worship all earth's noblest turn,
    Is neither Might nor Law alone, but both
Sphered in a Love that must for ever burn.

III.

Strange, in the heaven pure Pindar sang to be,
And that of John's unmastered mystery,
    Song should be symbol of all souls' delight
In quiring feast or by the crystal sea;—

And yet not strange, for ever since the dawn
Of life in leafy lair and river lawn,
  Young hearts have leaped in singing, and therewith
Round wintrier souls a wreathing sweetness drawn ;

From warble of bird to mightiest human tone,
A diapason, whose master-chord is one,
  · Runs, chiming with one harmony unheard,
Speech of all joy, and solace of all moan.

And he who hearkens not, and never heeds
When in his ear the charmèd utterance pleads,
  Is as a dead man, who beneath his turf
Sleeps deaf to all Spring's singing in her meads ;

And though bright blooms are breaking overhead,
Lies none the lightlier in his narrow bed ;
  And while Heaven's air throbs thick with richest
      song
May never taste Life's banquet round him spread.

Was it the hymn of worship or of war
That first broke silence in the years of yore ;
  Was melody born of a victor's boast,
Or trusting hearts that bowed their God before ?

Surely were it the joy of peace, not strife,
That first struck music on the strings of life ;
  The rose it is, and not the thorns, that yields
The scent that kings all sweets in spring-tide rife.

Woke that voice first to life in Indian woods,
Or in the lordlier mountain solitudes,
  Uprolling with the wreathing incense smoke
Where god-like calm for aye in azure broods?

Perchance, in seeking some one holy name
Beseeming Might forevermore the same,
  Men struck on earth that spark which was to be
Seed of an inextinguishable flame?

Maybe all music that the earth has known
Is but an echo from that ocean blown
  Which breaks upon this shoal of birth and death,
Whispering of isles and continents unknown;

So, as we scale majestic height past height
Of harmony, with all our soul's dear might,
  Each springing step lifts nearer to the land
Of matchless music and immortal light.

We know not whether it be so, or no;
Yet surely feel we, when our spirits flow
  With some divinest chord in unison,
Life were a mocking lure, if 'twere not so.

As song was deemed joy's soul in spheres above,
And harmony the law whereby they move,
  So through all crags of circumstance 'twere well
Our life leapt rhythmic to the law of love;

And sweetlier will the singing waters roll
For all the bitter battle-brunt they thole,
  As vanquished discord yields that master-chime
Which rounds mute music in one perfect whole.

For streams that spring from loftiest founts, and fall
In cataract over sheerest mountain wall,
  Weave them rich rainbows of their glittering
    wrack,
Robe their green glens in loveliest blossom-pall.

Better be scattered wide in sunlit spray
'Mid the pure peaks and golden glows of day,
  Than glide unruffled through rank lowlands, and
Be blackened in the world-thronged waterway.

Across the waste of years, a weary while,
Behind our path slow lengthening mile on mile,
  We wander lonely and companionless
Till heart meets heart and greets it with a smile;

Even as a journeying Arab, parched and worn,
Toils between skies that blaze and sands that burn,
  Till at the day's red end his weary eyes
Light on those groves and wells wherefor they yearn;

And with the palm-wings waving overhead,
Beneath, a couch of odorous herbage spread,
  Lying in calm delight he nigh forgets
Those many lifeless leagues he has to tread;

For all the toils he underwent before
His harbour in that blossoming islet's shore,
   Seem but the dusky frame wherein is set
A Heaven its gloom enhances evermore.

And rising ere the dawn lift on his way,
Freshly his heart, through all the withering day,
   Lies in the dews that fell on it erewhile
When he beside the bubbling waters lay.

Was it the Master argumentative,
Nursed in all wisdom that the world could give,
   Who out of his own human heart yet cried,
' Were't not for friendship, who would care to live?'

No thing to measure by mere social band,—
Caressing lip, or grasp of greeting hand ;
   But sudden sympathy from heart to eyes
Flashing of kindred souls that understand ;

Even as a beacon blaze from height to height
Leaps across leagues of lowland lulled in night,
   Whose misty bournes and slumbering thorps are
     blind
To track the passage of that pilgrim light.

May it not be, that as from simplest seeds
This manifold wonder of the world proceeds,
  From out the jarring faiths of all mankind
Will spring one worship that shall crown the creeds;

And so, as knowledge grows, and brotherhood,
And bloodshed dies i' th' kinship of all blood,
  From the old jangling strings shall rise at last
The grace of all earth's gladness in one Good?

Would we might see the dawning of that day;
Myriads of years, mayhap, will pass away
  Ere our eyes through far children's eyes behold
The roselight of that Easter ridge the gray;

And yet by self-surrender we may wing
The circling choir of centuries that bring
  Or soon or late one Morn of our desire
That all Earth's songsters sang and still shall sing.

'Tis likely, when light wreaths and wraiths of things
Come flocking for fit echo on the strings,
  That fingers oft should falter,—so of grace
Forgive the singer for the song he sings:

And if these notes seem nothing but the spray
Cast upward in some idle billow-play,
  Shut ye and shelve his weary book, and wend
With gladdened heart on some more gleeful way.

For not to every hearer's ear are sweet
The stammerings of a tongue that may repeat
   But one clear tone in changeful darkling guise,
And no one clothed in music that is meet.

KALLIRRHOE.

In old Pausanias, the voluble,
Lately I lit upon a tale of love,
Shining, a short sweet idyll, in his book,
As gleams in glittering quartz a vein of gold.
And this is how the traveller tells his tale :—

In Kalydon, by old Lycormas' stream
Hurrying his gold sands seaward evermore,
Lived long ago a maiden and a man.
Koresos, priest of Holy Dionyse,
Worshipped him daily with pure prayer, and when
The folk of Kalydon kept festival,
Held foremost office in the sacred hours.
Kallirrhoe—blue Dawn had looked on her
And kissed her sisterly, and oftentime
Had Helios swathed his splendour in a mist
To gaze with mellower glances in her eyes—
She, maiden sweetness of all Kalydon,
Turned lovelessly from Koresos away ;
And all his pleaded vows, and all the host

Of common acts by love made beautiful,
Seemed but to closer shut her heart to him.
At last, despairing, in a suppliant garb,
He laid his grief at Dionysos' feet,
Only beseeching him, the Beautiful,
To hear and help, if such should be his will.
Straightway a wonder lit on Kalydon ;
Strange madness seized the people, such as when
On the great festal day the Bacchic bands
Whirl dancing in a frenzy all divine.

They sent to far Dodona, where nightlong
The barefoot seers sat watching for a sign,
But nought was given until the third night came.
Then from the old prophetic oak they heard
Mysterious murmur, and the cauldron's clang ;
And with the morning came the oracle.
' The god was wroth, that faithful love and long
Should be so spurned and mocked in mere despite ;
His plague should tarry, till Kallirrhoe
Or other in her stead, be led and laid
A stainless offering on his altar-stone.'
Sadly the seekers turned to Kalydon,
To tell their story while the city wept.

But now the day was come, and all the hests
Of dark Dodona duly done, but one ;
Still there was none the fearful maiden found

Of all her kinsmen, who would die for her—
For father she had not, nor mother now—
And so, with laurel wreathèd in her hair
And draped in royal robe of sacrifice,
Pale, and her heavenly eyes with tears still wet,
She came, with mourning convoy virginal,
To Dionysos' altar and her death.

They bound, and on the altar laid the lamb
Devote to purge the plague of Kalydon,
And gave the knife and cup of holy wine
To Koresos—who bade the people pray
The god be pleased with willing sacrifice.
Then, casting light libation on his hair,
And quaffing, ' This be dedicate,' he cried,
' To Dionysos and to Love.'   Whereat
In his own heart he sheathed the knife, and sank
Breathless and smiling on the altar-stairs.
Then on the maiden came in mighty flood
The love that she had never known before,
And rich remembrance of those prayers of his
Unheeded, breathed at many eventides ;
And all her heart went out unto him dead.
' A perfect sacrifice !' the seers proclaimed,
Unbound and led her home—but longing love
Drew her, before on Kalydon the blush
Of dawn came crimson, and the city woke,

Where wells from shadowing rock a fountain forth
Hard by the haven's brink, therein to still
Forever all her griefs and her.   And so
The people gave the well another name,
And called it Fairest Flood, Kallirrhoe ;
And often, when a traveller stops to drink,
The white-haired fathers, while he rests him there,
Tell how a man for love once dared to die,
And how a maiden followed him in death ;
Adding that after, as the years went by,
The folk of Kalydon sent heralds forth
To far Dodona to the oracle ;
And how, when they had importuned the god
As to the lovers' lot, this answer came :
' Homeward return, and trouble me no more ;
Koresos and Kallirrhoe are well.'

LYKOPHRON.

IN happy Korinth, in the olden days;
When the great house of Kypselos had rule
In Periander, second lord, there fell
A mighty sorrow on people and on lord.
For he, the fameful chieftain, had two sons ;
The elder witless as a new-weaned child,
The younger keen and wise, and strong of soul.
And they, the heir and who the heir should be,
Going to Epidauros with a guard
To greet Lord Prokles there, their mother's sire,
Had met with warmest welcome, and had come
Back to fair Korinth and their father's hall
Amid all joyful clamour of the crowd.
But never, from that hapless hour till now,
Had Periander from his younger son
Got gleeful smile, or even a cloudless gaze ;
And him, the hope of each Korinthian heart,
Moving among his friends in mournful guise
And greeting courtesies with a desperate calm,

Had Periander in his rage forbid
The court, and every roof-tree of his peers,
Who yet received him gladly, when none saw.;
(For lord beloved of noble and of low,
Head of all youth at haughtiest contests he,
And crown of sunset cheer and festal song ;)
Whereat the tyrant bade his herald cry,
' Whoso hereafter shall be seen to speak
Or walk with Lykophron, or welcome him
Within his doors, shall pay Apollo's shrine
Ten talents as a holy penalty.'

Yet Lykophron grieved not thereat, nor sought
Of friend or fellow shelter any more,
But gliding sometime through the busy street
And market—trafficked in of all the world—
Alone and unaccosted, yet revered ;
And sometime in the shadeful avenue
Of porch or peristyle, he passed his days ;
Sleeping at night where chance had cast him down.

Lord Periander, as he one day came
Down to his townsfolk from the citadel,
Happened upon the selfsame portico
Where Lykophron lay foodless and unkempt ;
And seeing who was his darling once, so steeped
In misery, melted all the father's heart,

6

Crying with quivering lip, ' Wherefore dost thou,
Who might'st have had my wealth and realm in fee,
Choose rather a beggar's life ?   Implacable
Wert thou, if for—mischance that once befell,
Thou heap a bitterer on my hoary days.'
But no word answered Lykophron but this :
' Go, pay what penalty the god demands,
Having forbidden speech with one outlawed.'
And turned and calmly flung him down again.

So baffled Periander, hopeless now
Of any reconciliation, sent
Him with fit convoy to Korkyra's isle,
Whereover his rule stretched.   And year by year
The pale proud exile grew in love with all,
And Periander 'mid his gold grew grey
With grief.
                    For foolish Kypselos, beset
By many questions, turned this way and that,
At last had called to mind old Prokles' word,
Whispered at parting while they rode before :
' Know ye not, sons, whose hand your mother slew ?'
Which saying he laid not then to heart at all,
Not understanding.
                    But in Lykophron
The word had sunk, and split his heart in twain ;
For the old tale in Korinth widely went

That meek Melissa, lady of the land,
Had suddenly died in flower of all her days,
Just as her two bright buds had broken sheath ;
And no one knew how fate had fallen on her,
Of all who strewed the bier with blooms and tears.

And so slow Vengeance hovered, and then fell.
The light of life had set for Lykophron,
And bitter recollection of old crime
Stung Periander as a serpent's tooth.
In one mad fit of fury he had marched
Out, with a host of picked and seasoned men,
Laid siege to Epidauros, land and sea,
Starved her into surrender, battered down
Her towers, and taken grey-haired Prokles home,
To languish in dark walls his few faint days;
Yet never ease came to his heart thereby.
At last, sheer wanhope wearying strong pride
(Since now his old age lowered on him), he sent
Across the leaping blue to Lykophron,
Seeking return ; but he deigned not one word
Of answer. So maimed Hope drooped wing again.

When half a score of months was measured full,
And still no message came, bethinking him
Of what the sweetness of a sister's eyes

And pleading lips might work, he bade his one
Fair flower, and mirror of her mother lost,
Go with a reverend escort to that isle
Where lay his hope and heart.   So, dutiful,
She went ; and all the spirit of her house
Leapt to the deep blue eyes, as eagerly
She sought to win her brother back again ;
Telling of all the evil that would fall
If death should come, and the rich house be left
Prey to such wolves as whetted white teeth now
In Korinth—while he might unasked have all,
Did he but come, healing not ill with ill.
But never, he said, in Korinth would he step
So long as Periander lorded there.
So the sad maiden, sable-stoled, returned
Freighted with heavy tidings.
                                        Whereupon,
Periander, knowing retribution meet
For him had come, and he must yield to gods,
Sent forth the sacred herald of his house
(Who erst had served his father Kypselos,
What time he grasped the city's helm, and swept
Her weak and withered pilots to the sea)
With kingly gifts, and tender of all power
In Korinth, and the key of treasuries,
If he would come, and rule there in his stead ;
Himself resolved to yield up all, and bide

Henceforth upon the isle of crags, content.
And now, with few old lords that clung to him,
He waited in the harbour for a sign
(White ship-wings flapping in the broken breeze)
So he should pass, and Lykophron return ;
But when the long black hull dropped anchor there,
No lordly freight it bore, nor word, but this :

' The commons of Korkyra, when they knew
Their darling going, and the tyrant theirs,
Maddened to lose and maddened more to gain,
Had risen and slain him in their fear and love.'

So ancient Vengeance, ripening in due time,
Fruited to better fulness ; and thenceforth
The house of Kypselos, that had so high
Borne up its prow against all tides of fate,
Stooped on her whirling wheel to helpless fall.

DORNRÖSCHEN.

IT fell in time forgotten, far away,
When flood and field yet owned the fairy sway.

Glad were the folk, and glad the rose-red morn,
And glad was every bird that sang in thorn ;

For the fair boon so long besought had come,
And childish laughter lit the kingly home.

From every thorp and township, far and near,
The people came to taste the palace cheer.

And since the sweet one in Midsummer's glow
Was given, when loveliest roses bud and blow,

They called her Rosebud ; and the fairies whom
The King and Queen had bidden that day to come,

Showered on her all their gifts of luck and love ;
One gave her goodness, one a beauty above

All mortal maidens beautiful before ;
One wealth, one wisdom ; and—what could she
    more ?—

The last gave grace of lordly love unknown,
One day to come and clasp her for his own.

But one who dwelt far off, and was forgot,
Came at the last ; and albeit she might not

Undo the dower her sister fays had shed
So richly on the new-born golden head,

Shrieked, as she stamped her tiny foot in rage,
' She'll wound, ere she be sixteen years of age,

Her finger with a spindle, and so die.'
Then flew a raven out with boding cry.

The others might but murmur, through their tears,
' Not die, but slumber for a hundred years.'

Near sixteen summers fled, and Rosebud grew
More lovely with each dawn that lit the blue,

And kingly suitors thronged from every land
To win the peerless wonder of her hand.

Yet none the less her courteous cold disdain
Sent each one sorrowing toward his home again ;

It seemed her heart like a hid blossom lay
Waiting the glow of some yet unseen day.

It chanced one morning, left awhile alone
In that great vaulted chamber of her own,

She tired, and rambling through long corridors
And quaint forgotten rooms whose cumbrous doors

Swang after her with an ill-omened boom,
Came suddenly upon a turret room

Where sate a wee old woman spinning swift
White wool, that lay about in feathery drift,

With what to her seemed strangest thing on earth,
Who never had seen spindle since her birth.

Childlike, she begged to touch the golden thing,—
When all at once the chamber seemed to swing

Around her, and she sunk in slumber deep ;
And with her all the castle slept that sleep.

Straightway around it, says the olden tale,
There sprang a hedge of thorn-boughs like a pale;

Higher than tallest poplar tops it grew,
And past its rampart no bird ever flew.

Many a Prince from far away was fain
To break the magic circle—but in vain;

The thorn trees clasped him round with cruel arms,
And few 'scaped free with less than deathly harms.

So that the fearful fame of it flew wide
And scared all comers from the country side.

* * * * *

A hundred winters now were come and past,
And of a hundred summers shone the last.

One morning broke so brightly, 'mid such glee
Of bird-throats thrilled from blossoming tree to
 tree,

And such a flowerful fragrance in the air,
Folk said no day had ever dawned so fair.

All life seemed flushed with gladness to the brim,
And even the threatening thorns looked not so grim.

That day a knightly traveller, passing by,
Halted his horse the enchanted castle nigh ;

He heard the greybeard fathers tell the tale,
Then straightway doffed his helm and glittering
    mail ;

And a strange gladness seemed to surge and sing
Within him, as he reached the fairy ring.

Thorns changed to flowering laurels, as he pressed
His way through that deep thicket's yielding breast,

And white and blue and golden blossoms sprang
Beneath his feet, and loud before him sang

One bird of plumage wonderful, who seemed
Guiding him where the castle's darling dreamed.

Across the court, and through still corridors
Flew on the bird ; and as he flew, the doors

Swang wide before them noiselessly, till they
Reached the high turret room where Rosebud lay.

She seemed but newly fallen asleep ; an air
Of summer from the casement stirred her hair,

And shadowed sunlight fell thro' vine-veiled bars
Around her wreath of lily and jasmine stars,

And lit the beauty bathed wherein she lay
Like a shut blossom waiting for the day.

Soft sang the bird ; the kneeling knight beside
Lift to his lips one white hand of his bride,

When suddenly oped the heaven of her eyes
And smiled upon him with a glad surprise ;

And rose-lips murmured, ' Wherefore, love, so long
Wert thou a coming ?' Whereupon the song

Of that strange bird rang wondrously through all
The castle—and King awoke in council hall,

Suitors awoke who sought his justice there,
And boy and man ; and 'mid her garden fair

Awoke the Queen, while all her maidens round
Stirred from their slumbering on the lawny ground ;

And the great clock, clanging the hour of noon,
Woke the old echoes from their century's swoon.

All sounds of life grew busy, and the din
Of making and of moiling hummed within.

That summer noon the lordliest and the least
Kept Rosebud's birthday and her bridal feast ;

For strong love born to break the spell was come,
And elfin laughter lit the kingly home.

SHELLEY.

'The prophetic soul
Of the wide world dreaming on things to come.'

THE world was old and dying, and the gloom
  Of long life fading held an iron sway
Upon the sunless ether ; for the doom
  Foreshadowed in her weary past, hung grey
And ghostlike on her wan and wasted strand,
    And spirits that had filled her prime
    With mighty melodies sublime,
Were past for aye and faded, lost in wastes of time,
  Gilding the sunlight of a sweeter land ;
    Leaving all lustre of their mortal name
Close-cherished in the worn and ancient hand
    Of Earth their mother, an undying flame ;
But now all beauty and melodious chime
  Were dead and silent, and a living shame
  Crept on the world and hid the lustre of their fame ;

When suddenly, with an upspringing flame
  Like lightning from the mist-enshrouded hills,
Thy tameless universal spirit came
  Into the gloom as the sun comes that fills
The heavy drift of dawn with orient blaze ;
      And through the heapèd clouds that hung
      Above the fainting earth, thy song
Broke forth in pealing thunder-echoes, worldward
    flung,
  And threw the clear calm light of olden days,
    The shadeless glories of the days to come,
  Upon thy mother Earth ; and then the haze
    That so long had becanopied our home,
The deep-set sorrows that the world's heart wrung,
  Stole with still footsteps to their ancient gloom,
  To lie for ever wrapt in a forgotten tomb.

Flushed with the fire of old Philosophy,
  Earth's supreme aureole in the primal years,
Bent thou thine inly-thrilling prophet eye
  Past all the strife, the craven doubts and fears
That thicketed our common earth with weeds,
      And in the rich supernal glow
      Of thoughts that from the world's heart flow
Into the looming future fraught with weal or woe,
  .And all the hopes that spring from thought-set
    seeds,

Thou centredst all thy young life's blossoming;
Facing all fury of the hateful creeds
That sought to numb thee with their venomed
sting
And stay the mighty spirit's riverflow ;
Cleaving thy clear way with unwearied wing
Through world-wide wastes of bitter tears and
sorrowing ;

But not in thy heart, O strong bird of gladness,
Lingered for long time any shaft of pain ;
Flashing from grief-clouds, with a thunderous
madness
Rich rolling round thee, sang thou yet again,
Storming the calm heights of thy spirit's world
With so intensely sweet a strain
That listening is almost pain ;
Flooding our nature over as rich thunder-rain
Floods the parched meadows whereon it is hurled
From off the lead-cliffs of a cloudy land ;
Curling in white wrath as great waves are curled
In the wild might of ocean's angry hand,
Fierce-breaking on a bleak and lonely main ;
Songs that shall break forever, amid Love's
band,
Upon the bluffs of ages and the world's wide
sand.

But now, enfolded in the clear white glow
  Solemnly flooding all Eternity,
Throughout whose shadeless deeps upthronging flow
  The never-ending heart-sprung harmony,
The soul-outpouring of the stars of thought,
    Far past all touch of bitter tears,
    All bale and dole of earthborn years,
A sunlike soul thou gleamest 'mid thy starry peers ;
  Winging that song Earth comprehended not
    While thine own present spirit she possessed ;
  That sea-flood depth of tone that sages sought
    In olden time to summon at their hest,
Now rolls its rich diapason on their ears,
  Now casts a flameful beauty on their rest,
  Breaking in mazy volume from one mastering
    breast.

Some veiling dimness shrouds thee from our eyes,
  And mindful sorrow floods them deep with tears;
Grey gulfs of ocean tempest-wrought arise
  Like some weird vision of our night-fed fears,
Green-gleaming bitter surges, whirlwind-driven,
    Rich with the thunder of white death,
    Blasting with their sea-cold breath
All the bright morning promise of the young bud's
    sheath ;

But that dear outflow of supreme song given
   To be thine everlasting aureole,—
  That crowning joy of all the glow of Heaven,
   Shrined is for ever with thy stainless soul ;
And blazing from afar, like stars on death,
  That strange deep songtide roars in Titan-roll,
  Filling far worlds of love beneath thy heart's
    control.

REQUIESCAS IN PACE.

In Memoriam, A. E. P. ob. April, 1876.

YEA, thou may'st wander far on gleaming strands
Drenched in primeval azure, on the sands
Of that fair covert where thy shadow lies,
Thrown like rich sunglow ; while o'er thee uprise
Great shapes of strange calm beauty, and gaze upon
Thy trancèd form, filling awhile thy lone
And barren sleeping with some golden dream,
Flushed in the moon of sadness, and the gleam
Of old-world glories that are living still ;
Still, still they live : the ages pass and fill
The limbo of Time with overgone regrets,
But their sun-orb of beauty never sets—
Even now is shedding his immortal beams
Upon thy spirit's face, where, lapt in dreams
And starry thoughts of aught may thee betide
In that rich kingdom, thou dost stilly bide

The eve of future splendours and delights.
Surrounding thee with curious eyes the sprites
Of that rare country watch thy sleeping face,
And wiping fondly from thine eyes all trace
Of pain-wrought passing tears, embalm thy head
In deathless odours, drawn from blooms that shed
Their ever-vernal sweetness through that land.
And thou, deep-sleeping, hearest not the grand
Uprising choral harmony from far,
That rears rich billows to the ocean star,
And floods the faery woods that environ
Thy dreamful resting-place, with singing moan ;
Songs that were born in elder worlds, and rose
Triumphantly from silent deathlike close
Ere those old times were ended, echo now ;
Over thy head they stay their streaming flow,
And heap their throbbing pulses on thy brain ;
But still thou heed'st them not, in vain, in vain
Their chordings tremulous intoxicate
With volumed sweetness all who listening wait
Till thy long slumber shall be past for aye.
Still, as the dawn-glow blossoms into day,
And night's dun shadows fade in air and die,
Yet richer scenes and rarer meet thine eye
So deeply sunk in weary sleep, and pain
Not yet enloosened from thy heart and brain ;
And starry eyes are bent on thine, and gleam

Through veiling tears, from far blue depths that
    seem
The morning-flooded vistas that uplead
The soul to that far heaven enshadowèd
Beyond the love that drowns their nearer glow ;
And haply in the joy of that dreamflow
Thy thirsting spirit may find restful calm,
And drinking in the dear and healing balm
Of that sweet presence, may enfolded lie
For ever in love's immortality.

ÆTAS NOVA.

NEW-COMING years had borne the old away
Into the glooming shadows of dead Time,
And Life was young, fresh-born, and rich in joy.
Strife, clanging discontent, and sickly hate
Had sunk beneath the load of springing love
And friendliness, now blossoming in their stead ;
Still, faint remembrance of the dark time gone
Lingered in human hearts, and from their gloom
Made the new ages richer in their eyes.
Old gods were gone ; and in the garden-world
They were gods only, who brought deeper hues
Of beauty, grander bursts of supreme tone,
And spread and poured them forth for human weal.
Glad-eyed as children, filled with power of joy
Beyond all highest craving of the past,
They trod the old earth glorying, and saw
Through the calm night shot through with trembling
    stars

The swift still rush of planets like their own,
Whirl-hurried round the centre-blaze of fire ;
Broad homes of happy life, on earth, in air,
Or basking in rich caverns of blue sea ;
Deep-drenched in orange dawn, or growing grey
Beneath the blood-red blaze of setting suns ;
And teeming through with life hues, like their
    own;—
Greeting and parting, evermore beheld
Each in his fellow's eyes gleam deep and wide
The sunfire of that gladness that had fallen,
Free from all stain, fresh on the newer age.

OCEAN-IDYLL.

THE tempest is singing
  A song that ends never,
And tones of emotion
  Are borne on its breast ;
Fresh harmonies flinging
  With wildest endeavour
Their light o'er the ocean,
  Sink into their rest.

White seabirds are winging
  Their way through dark weather,
In wild wheeling motion
  Each one to his nest ;
Around them is clinging,
  And binds them together,
Impassioned emotion
  The storm has impressed

On birdlike affections
　　Upsprung in the heart
That beats in bird-bosoms
　　So blithe and so free ;—
And spray-built erections,
　　Gleam tinted with dart
Of bright scaly blossoms
　　Upshot from the sea,

Are rising and falling,
　　Are sparkling with light,
In Even's rich gloaming
　　That's shadowed by cloud,
And voices are calling
　　That rise o'er the night,
Of ocean-birds homing
　　And singing aloud.

CHILDHOOD.

GLAD in the glowing
   Light of their spring,
Child-hearts in laughter
   Ripple and ring ;
Happy, not knowing
   What may befall
In that Hereafter,
   When the leaves fall.

Now are the roses
   Buds but to see,
Mosses yet wreathing
   Blossom and tree ;
As each uncloses,
   Seem we to hear
In its still breathing,
   Song swelling near;—

Chords that were sounding
    Ere the world was,
Where the Immortals
    Pass and repass ;
Where by the bounding
    River of gold,
Far through pearl portals,
    Fold beyond fold,

See we that splendour
    Whence we are come,
Love like light living
    Here in her home ;
High, yet so tender,
    In each bright birth
Working and weaving
    Gladness on earth !

So in the singing
    Days of our dawn,
Heaven's veiling glory
    Round us yet drawn,
See we no springing
    Sorrow or strife,
Know but one story,
    Lovely is Life !

SONNETS.

SONNETS.

I.

APRIL TWILIGHT.

IT is a calm sweet evening ; the orbèd moon,
  Luscious with a pale golden springtide glow,
  Is rising solemnly, patient and slow ;
  Dusk shades are falling fast, and soon, full soon,
Night will brood cloud-clad on the sleeping town,
  Darkness will cover all its weal and woe ;
  But for those hearts that ever ebb and flow
  In unison with Nature, and, alone,
Feel the companionship of the great world
  Throbbing with all the burden of her soul,
  Is endless hope and sunshine in the night,
As through those thunder-vapours that are hurled
  Together with an aëry organ-roll,
  Breaks evermore the lightning of delight.

II.

SEPTEMBER STORM.

BUT even now fierce rain was beating fast
  Upon the shivering woodlands, and the cry
  Of southern winds fresh from captivity
  Still echoed on the regions overpast ;
But few short moments gone, the autumn blast
  Of torrid ether rent the cloudful sky,
  Dashed through its leaden mountains heapèd
    high,
  And flashing torrents from their ruins cast ;
Yet now all strife is over, lulled and gone
  For aye to rumble on through Arctic seas,
Red floods of sunset burst, as fresh as dawn,
  From the bright King of planet emperies,
And pale blue heavens gleam from rain-clouds torn,
  Fair and untroubled in their maiden peace.

III.

WORLD'S WOE.—I.

O FOR a wind to roll this fog away;
    These dreary mists that pitilessly hide
    The clear deep sky of truth, home where abide
Life, Love, and Beauty in immortal day!
Sages have had sweet glimpses, in the grey
    Gone ages, of that everlasting tide
    Of light celestial, the ocean wide
Of Heaven broad-breaking on the mortal clay;
And have awakened from the blissful dream,
    Full of fresh fervour from its glamouring,
    And writ rapt records, in prophetic tone
Of mighty verse, that to our senses bring
    Some scent of thymy hills in sunset gleam,
    Where mused those grey bards at night fall, alone.

IV.

WORLD'S WOE.—II.

But no ! that time again may never be ;
  'Twas but the changing glory of a dream
  Fallen on their eyes with the rich even beam,
  And is lost now to all futurity ;
Clearer and colder visions we are to see ;
  Straining our weak sight thro' the riven seam
  Of Night, and Nature's dark immensity,
  And through that vaster gulf that parts the stream
Of conscious being from a lifeless sea,
  Chill cavern-solitude yawns on our sense
  And boundless Death breaks in upon our eyes,
Yearning to see some glorious vision rise ;
  We sink to mother Earth in sorrow, whence
  Our soul upsprang unto Infinity.

V.

IN THE ISLE OF WIGHT.

Passing from one high overhanging shade
   Of rocky bluffs bare of all herb or tree,
   We gain a valley sloping to the sea
Blue glancing in the sheer sunlight that played
Over the waves like a rich diamond braid ;
   Haunted by a far-murmuring melody,
   The echo of wave-plash waft from that bright sea,
Summer air surges freshly overhead,
Immersing all sense in a dreamful flow
   Of fantasies unutterably sweet,
   That seem to home them in that mornlit vale ;
And save the flashing of the seabirds fleet,
   Circling around us with their mournful wail,
   The clear blue heaven is one unbroken glow.

VI.

HASTINGS.

A CLUSTER of red roofs deep in the cleft
  Of seaward shouldering bluffs, to eastward strown
  With gorse and grazing herds, treeless and brown;
To westward crowned with all that Time has left
In dim remembrance of that Norman theft
  That flung free Hastings 'neath the feudal frown,
  Grey broken walls that echo the renown
Of him who England from her children reft.

Now quiet is here, and hushed for evermore
  Is all the din, and pale and dead the pride
  And blaze of antique pomp and chivalry,
And halls that, hanging on the southern shore,
  Once rang with passionate song from side to side,
  Ring only to the tempest and the sea.

VII.

HASTINGS.

DEAR town of ruddy roofs and dwellings olden
 And mazy ways from winding street to street,
 How fresh thou look'st in thy hale age, to greet
The summer flush of sunrise falling golden!
Rooted so sure 'twixt bluffs to east and west,
 That tower out seaward as 'twere to enclose
 Thy populous haven from all winds but those
That speed thy weary fishers home to rest;

Bearing on stormbeat strand the memories
 Of broader traffic, and a richer throng
 Of warriors mailed and merchants in thy midst,
And sometime pomp of joust and festal song;
 But joying now, as then thou never didst,
 In naught but peaceful toil and fruits of peace.

VIII.

Ψυχή.

ONE morning, in the young year's early days,
 When Earth lay locked in January cold,
 We saw a butterfly flit, free and bold
As 'twere midsummer, thro' the shimmering haze
Broken only by the winter sun's sick blaze,
 That ruthlessly from ocean on us rolled—
 A harvest thing of dun and dusky gold
Belated by the lure of timeless rays.

So, in the mists of being, might a soul
 Untimely born into an alien air,
 Stray shivering in that life's chill fog and foam ;
And though all tides of trouble round it roll,
 Yet on its way in hope still bravely bear,
 Rich with the roseflush of its summer home.

IX.

MAY MORNING.

O MAY, thou smiler on unnumbered years,
  Bright blue-eyed harbinger of Summer's glow,
  Crowner of all the springtime's tender flow,
Welcome wert thine, even hadst thou come in tears ;
Coming as now thou comest, free from fears,
  Far banishing all thought of want or woe,
  Thou seem'st both harbinger and angel now,
And Nature gladdens as thy presence nears.

Why should our hearts be thankless, voices still ?
  Thou art as kind and lovely as of yore ;
Why, when our fathers welcomed thee in hill
And plain with pomp of village festival,
  Joying the more as they praised thee the more,
  Should we not hail thee, dearest month of all ?

X.

RALPH WALDO EMERSON.

(D. 27 April, 1882.)

DEAR Emerson, thy name can never die
  While there are souls to kindle, hearts to warm ;
  Its casual mention shall call up a swarm
Of thoughts that deepest in our nature lie ;
Shall wake the brooding world of memory
  To life and music,—shower down softest balm
  On stormtost souls aye thirsting for that calm
That reigned divinely in thy heart and eye ;

Brother of ours, and universal Earth,
  Strong seer into supremest mysteries,
  The human heart of hope that beat in thee,
To us who are the kinsmen of thy birth
  Shall never cease to beat in sympathy,
  And speak to ours in bird and flower and breeze.

XI.

STOKE POGIS.

A LOWLY grey old church all ivy-grown
  Amid a waving elm-grove hid away,
    Where through legendic panes the rich lights
      play
On age-worn floor and many a storied stone ;
Even such a solitude as singer lone,
  Deep brooding on the night of our brief day,
  Might love to linger in, when evening grey
Stole over to the woodland wind's low moan ;

Haunted by memory of him who wrought
  For all the years his sober song and sweet,
  Stretched under yonder yew tree's solemn shade,
This resting-place shall evermore be sought
  Of them that love to tread where paced his feet,
  Where round them rings the music that he made.

XII.

MARLOW.

A SWEET shy hamlet bosomed in elm-bowers
   Where sirens of all feather sing and sleep,
   Whereround wood-shrouded hills forever keep
Calm watch through noontide and through mid-
     night hours ;
A river lordliest in this land of ours
   Slow winding past the fields white mowers reap
   And bloomy meadow banks where willows weep
Beside their mossgrown graves and ivy towers;—

That lowly home where he, the lord of love
   And singing, whom all Life knew for her own,
   Spent months of toil and sorrow and sometime
     peace ;
Of whom all breathes—his beechen woods above,
   The soft lawns meadowsweet and clover strown,
   The lilied river asleep beneath its trees.

XIII.

AUTUMN.

WHEN mild October, close on harvest time,
    Comes lengthening twilight and delaying dawn,
    And bathes in colder dews each dell and lawn,
And strips the woodland of its withering prime ;
When brown leas bear a boding touch of rime,
    And the brave lark thrills heavenward at mid-
        morn
His loud last song, before that tempest-borne
Far faring of him to some sunnier clime;—

The old Earth knows her winter is at hand ;
    And clasping close her happy autumn-sheaves,
And rich in promise of her seeded land,
    Rests, with a wreath of rose and russet leaves
On her brown brow light-lying, lone and grand,
    Biding the Dark that ripens while it reaves.

XIV.

' L'amor che muove 'l Sole e l'altre stelle.'

So calm a morning does not often shine
　　On autumn woods and fields of glimmering dew;
　　'Aloft the sun thrills in his heavenly blue,
Below all earth lies bathed in bliss divine ;
No ripple breaks the river's radiant line,
　　No rustle creeps the grey-haired willows through;
Rings only, out of throats of many a hue,
The mirth of hearts fresh fired with Nature's wine ;

Steals only, in all breath of earth and heaven,
　　An undertone our souls are dull to hear
Of that high song once heard through spheres love-
　　　　riven
　　By one who woke and wrote in joy and fear ;
Ah, not as unto him to us is given
　　To meet such music with unclouded ear !

XV.

SUNWARD.

WESTWARD we walked, to see the setting sun ;
  A balmy breath of evening round us blew,
  And tenderest saffron flushed the sky, where-
      through
Light clouds like golden threads shot one by one;
As the sun sank, a rose-red splendour won
  Upon the purpling west ; the glory grew ;
  Soft carols from the branches rang anew
As though the morning were but now begun ;—

One silver sickle in the fields of light
  Hung over yellow harvest heaps below,
And slowly on wide wings uprose the Night ;
  Still in the western heaven that gracious glow
Lingered in deeper crimson, till the bright
  Stars leapt forth, and Day's pulses ceased to flow.

Elliot Stock, Paternoster Row, London

www.ingramcontent.com/pod-product-compliance
Lightning Source LLC
Chambersburg PA
CBHW031157050726
47495CB00019B/2464